CATHERINE ROBINSON

Hullaballoony

Illustrated by Tony Kenyon

MACDONALD YOUNG BOOKS

Chapter One

Hullaballoony moved in to Joe's house the day Mum brought Henry home from the hospital.

"Say hello to Henry," Mum said to Joe. "He's your new brother – look!"

Joe looked. He didn't see any new brother. He could only see a small face, red and wrinkled and wrapped in a snowy-white blanket. He pulled a face.

"That's not a brother," he said, in a cross voice. "You said I'd have a brother to play with. That can't *play* with me!"

Mum laughed. "Darling, he's only a baby – of course he can't play with you yet. But he will, when he's older. You'll see."

That was when Hullaballoony arrived. A mean, nasty little voice whispered in Joe's ear. It was Hullaballoony's voice, only Joe didn't know that yet. *I don't like it*, said the voice. *Take it back.*

"I don't like it," said Joe, clearly. "Take it back." Mum laughed again. It was a slightly wobbly laugh. "Henry's not an 'it', darling," she said.

"He's a little boy, just like you," said Dad. "Just look at him – he's lovely."

"No, he's not," muttered Hullaballoony, in Joe's voice. "He's horrible. I don't want him."

The next day, Granny came to visit. Joe
ran to the door to greet her.

"Hello, Granny," he said.

"Where's this new little brother, then?"
said Granny, looking for Henry.

"It's nice to see you, Granny," said Joe.

"Oh, look at the little pet!" said Granny.
"Who's a little darling, then?" She pulled
down a fold of the snowy-white blanket
and smiled at the baby.

Joe tugged at Granny's sleeve. "Look Granny, look at my painting!"

"He's got your eyes," Granny told Mum.

"I painted it for you," Joe said to Granny.

"And I can see he's got your nose," Granny told Dad.

"Specially for you," said Joe.

"And I think," said Granny, "I really do think – is that my mouth he's got?"

"GRANNY!" shouted Joe, very loudly.

Mum, Dad and Granny all looked at him in surprise. Inside the blanket, Henry began to cry.

"Joe!" said Mum.

"You've woken the baby," scolded Dad.

Granny sat Joe on her knee and explained in a kind voice that he must never, ever shout so close to Henry. She told him that it would frighten the baby and make him cry.

"Now," she said. "Now show me your picture. What is it – is it your new baby brother?"

"No," said Joe. "It's a monster. A big fat monster. He's got Mummy's eyes and Daddy's nose and your mouth, and his name is Hullaballoony."

"I see," Granny said. "Hullaballoony. And is he very frightening?"

"No," said Joe. "Not to me. He's my friend."

Chapter Two

And so it proved to be. Wherever Joe
went, Hullaballoony went too. At
mealtimes a place had to be laid for him.

"Hullaballoony can't eat fish fingers,"
Joe explained. Or, "Hullaballoony doesn't
like porridge."

And so Mum got some cheese on toast
instead, or cornflakes, which Joe helped
Hullaballoony to eat.

Whenever they went to the park, Mum
pushed Henry in the pram, and Joe pulled
Hullaballoony on a piece of string.

"Come along, Joe," Mum said. "It's cold. Don't walk so slowly."

"It's not me," said Joe, twirling the string. "It's Hullaballoony. His little legs can't keep up. He's tired."

At bathtime, Hullaballoony made a fuss about having his hair washed, and spat the toothpaste on to the bathroom floor because he didn't like the taste.

"Joe," said Mum, "I'm warning you."

"It's not me," said Joe. "Hullaballoony likes strawberry, not mint. If you bought him strawberry he wouldn't spit."

At bedtime, Hullaballoony demanded three extra stories, or ten kisses, five on each cheek.

"More," said Joe. "More stories. More kisses."

"That's enough now," said Dad, kissing the air where Hullaballoony's face was. "It's time for sleep."

Joe threw himself on to his side, away from Dad and sulked.

"Hullaballoony's not tired," he muttered.

Sometimes Henry's crying in the night woke Joe. And Hullballoony too, of course. Joe would have gone straight back to sleep, but Hullaballoony wouldn't let him. *You cry too,* he whispered inside Joe's head. *Tell them you've got a pain. Tell them you feel sick. Tell them you're thirsty.*

So Mum would feed Henry while Dad ran around with medicine and buckets and juice for Joe, and in the morning they would all look awful and feel worse.

All except Henry, who was a happy, smiley baby, and Hullaballoony, who never got tired.

Nobody ever saw Hullaballoony, of course. Not Mum or Dad, or Granny, or the man at the paper shop who always gave Joe striped humbugs from a jar.

"Not humbugs," said Joe, kicking the counter, "Bubble gum."

"Not bubble gum," said Mum firmly, as she paid for her newspaper. "It's very kind of Mr Evans to give you anything at all."

"It's not for me," Joe explained. "It's for Hullaballoony. He hates humbugs."

"I see," said Mr Evans, looking puzzled.

Mum went pink. "It's humbugs or nothing, Joe, I'm afraid."

"Nothing, then," whispered Joe, and kicked the counter again. "Nothing, nothing, nothing. So there."

Not even Joe could see Hullaballoony, but he knew he was there. He was always there. He never went away.

Chapter Three

One day, Mum was feeding Henry.

"Mum," said Joe, "Hullaballoony is hungry."

Mum glanced at the clock on the mantelpiece. "Already?" she said. "You've only just had lunch."

"Not me," said Joe quickly. "Hullaballoony. He's thirsty too."

"Hullaballoony's just had lunch, as well. Shepherd's pie and a big piece of chocolate cake," Mum reminded Joe. She sighed. "I'll get you something when I've finished with Henry.

"Not when you've finished. *Now*," Joe insisted.

"No, Joe. I'm feeding Henry. You'll just have to wait."

But Joe didn't want to wait. He whined and moaned. He lay on the carpet and kicked his legs about, and all the time Henry sucked happily on.

"Joe," said Mum, crossly. "You are being *very* silly."

Just then, Hullaballoony spoke in Joe's ear. Joe listened thoughtfully. He picked himself up from the floor.

"I'll get it," he told Mum. "Juice and a biscuit. I can get that." And he went into the kitchen.

Mum called to him to be careful, but he didn't listen. He got out the juice from the fridge. He sloshed it into two cups, one for him, one for Hullaballoony. A lot of it splashed on to the floor. Even more of it spilled down his T-shirt.

He got out the biscuits from the
cupboard. They were chocolate biscuits,
in a tin. Joe took off the lid and grabbed a
handful.

"Yum, yum," said Hullaballoony, inside
Joe's head. "Lots for me. Lots and lots."

Joe crammed biscuits into his mouth,
and wiped his hands on his front.

"What are you doing, Joe?" called Mum
from the sitting-room. "Come in here,
please."

What are you doing, Joe?

Joe went in, and Mum looked at him.
She looked at his mouth, stuffed with
biscuits. She looked at the spilt juice and
chocolate fingerprints down his front.

"It wasn't me," said Joe, quickly. "It was Hullaballoony."

Mum was silent for quite a long time. "I'm not sure I like Hullaballoony," she said at last.

Joe wasn't sure he liked him any more, either. He was always making people cross, or getting Joe into trouble. The problem was, Hullaballoony didn't seem to want to go away.

Chapter Four

A new family was moving into the house
next door. Joe stood and watched. The
new family had a piano, and a big roll of
red carpet, patterned with gold.

They had crates and crates of books, and a parrot in a cage. They also had a little girl about Joe's size and a baby a bit bigger than Henry. He ran around the garden on unsteady, fat dimpled legs.

The next morning, Mum and Joe and Henry took a cake to the the new neighbours.

"How kind," said the lady next door. "We love cake, don't we Daisy?"

Joe's mum and Daisy's mum went into the kitchen to drink coffee, and Joe and Daisy were sent into the garden to play.

"What's your baby called?' Daisy asked Joe.

"Henry," Joe told her.

"Ours is called Max," said Daisy.

"Babies don't do much, do they?" said Joe, gloomily

"Not much," Daisy agreed. "But Max is better now he can walk. He's more fun. I can play with him now." She looked at Joe. "What shall we do then?"

Joe shrugged, and looked down at the grass. "Don't care."

"Don't you want to play with me?" Daisy stared at him.

"It's not that."

Then Joe looked up at Daisy. Suddenly he found himself explaining to her about Hullaballoony, about how he sometimes made Joe do and say things he never really meant to do or say.

"Oh," said Daisy. "And is he here now?"

"Course he is," Joe said glumly. "He's always here."

Daisy looked at the air next to Joe's right shoulder, the exact spot where Hullaballoony's eyes were.

"Now look," she said firmly. "Joe's going to play with me now."

"You can play too if you like," Daisy said. "I don't mind. But I don't want you being a pest. D'you understand?"

Joe and Daisy played together every day after that. They made dens in the bushes. They had picnics on the lawn.

They played football on the drive, and pirates around the pond.

Sometimes Max brought his toys out to play with them, and when Henry began to walk he joined them, too.

"Do you know," said Joe's mum one day. "I haven't seen anything of Hullaballoony lately."

"Oh no," said Joe. "He's not my friend any more. Daisy is. Hullaballoony's gone away." And the funny thing was, he never came back.

Look out for more exciting titles in the Storybook series:

Mog and Bumble by Catherine Robinson
Mog was Sarah's cat. He was just an ordinary tabby, but to Sarah he was beautiful. When Bumble arrived – a soft-looking puppy with one floppy ear – Mog was furious. He hissed fiercely every time he saw Bumble. Then Mog disappeared…

Emily's Legs by Dick King-Smith
At first, nobody noticed Emily's legs. Then, at the Spider Sports, everyone began to ask questions.

Carla's Magic Dancing Boots by Leon Rosselson
Carla loves her new golden boots – they are sparkly and special. But the next day at school her friends laugh at her. Carla is unhappy until Grandma shows her that the boots are magic – magic dancing boots…

Maxie's Music by Elizabeth Dale
Maxie loves playing music, and the louder the better. But her family don't appreciate her talent. Not until one very exciting night when Maxie's musical gift makes her a hero.

Gilly the Kid by Adèle Geras
Gilly the Kid is a cowgirl. She can round up cattle, throw a lasso and ride faster than anyone south-west of Coyote Canyon. But what she'd like to do is catch some real live baddies.

All these books and many more in the Storybook series can be purchased from your local bookseller. For more information about Storybooks, write to: *The Sales Department, Macdonald Young Books, 61 Western Road, Hove, East Sussex BN3 1JD.*